Weird and Wacky Plants

by Becky Manfredini

PHOTOGRAPHY CREDITS: 3 (b) Buddy Mays/Corbis; 4 (b) ©Joel Sartore/Getty Images; 5 (tr) Artville/Getty Images; 6 (t) ©Stephen Shepherd/The Garden Picture Library/Getty Images; 7 (b) ©shapencolour/Alamy Images; 8 (b) ©Geoffrey Bryant/Science Source/Photo Researchers, Inc.; 9 (r) ©Ben Cooper/ Documentary Value/Corbis; 10 (r) ©Reuters/Corbis; 11 (b) ©Roberto Soncin Gerometta/Lonely Planet Images/Getty Images

Printed in Mexico

ISBN: 978-0-544-07237-4

10 0908 20 19 18 17

4500669231 A B C D E F G

Contents

Vocabulary

seed flower
root stem
leaf cone
fruit

Stretch Vocabulary

lobes
nectar
succulent

Introduction

Plants grow from seeds. They have features that allow them to survive. Some plants have weird and wacky features that allow them to survive, too.

Kudzu can harm or kill other plants. Kudzu can easily grow 12 inches (30 centimeters) a day. Their roots can weigh 400 pounds (181 kilograms)! The roots are the part of a plant that holds the plant in place.

Kudzu's nickname is "the vine that ate the South."

Trapping Insects

Watch out, insects! You may be trapped by a Venus flytrap. A leaf is the part of a plant that makes food for the plant. Each leaf on this plant has a pair of spiny jaws called lobes. Venus flytrap leaves attract insects with nectar, a liquid that smells sweet. The jaws close around insects when they rest on the lobe. The lobe can shut in less than a second!

The plant sets its trap on sunny days.

Like a Star

Its real name is carambola.

What is juicy and crunchy and shaped like a star? It is star fruit! You know that a fruit is the part of a plant that holds seeds. The star fruit grows on a bushy tree. The tree's flowers are a pinkish lavender color. A flower is the plant part that makes seeds. The fruit can taste a little sour and a little sweet. You might think of a plum, a lemon, and a pineapple when you bite into it.

This plant grows well in warm, wet weather.

Giant Leaves

You can not eat this plant, but you can stand under its leaves. Any one leaf will give you and your family shade on a hot, sunny day! This plant grows fast. Its stalk, or stem, grows to about as tall as a grown man. A stem is the part of a plant that holds it up. The plant's leaves are even bigger than its stem.

A Rock, or Not?

Put this plant next to some rocks and you would not think it is alive. Looking like a rock protects the plant from getting eaten by animals. Animals might not know this is a plant!

This plant lives in hot, dry deserts. It has succulent, or juicy, leaves. The juicy leaves keep the plant alive when it is hot and dry outside.

This plant comes in many patterns and colors.

Do Not Sit Under This Tree!

Pine trees are tall. They smell nice, too. But do not sit under this pine tree. It has huge cones! A cone is the part of a non-flowering plant that holds the plant's seeds. This kind of pine tree has the largest cones. Some cones can be more than one foot (30 centimeters) long. They can weigh more than five pounds (two kilograms)!

These pine trees grow in some parts of California.

Beware of Teddy Bear

From a distance, this plant looks like a teddy bear. It seems to have fuzzy arms like a teddy bear. Beware! Up close, you can see that this cactus has sharp, silvery spines. Do not touch the spines. They can hurt!

This plant grows flowers and fruit. It grows well in hot, dry deserts.

jumping cholla or teddy bear cholla

It Is Stinky!

This is one of the largest blooming plants in the world. People travel from many places to see it. Most people will never see the plant bloom, or open up. And it is stinky! The plant's smell attracts insects. When the plant blooms, the flower lasts only a couple of days.

This plant comes from a rain forest.

It Might Walk, or Not!

This palm tree is different from other trees. Most trees have one trunk with underground roots. Look at this palm tree. It looks as if it has many little roots, or legs above the ground. Some people think that it can walk because it can grow new roots around old roots. But it can not really walk. It does not talk either!

This tree grows in rain forests.

Draw and Write!

Draw a picture of your favorite weird and wacky plant from this book. Write a short paragraph about it. Tell why it is your favorite plant.

Make a Picture Book

Use the Internet or another source. Find information about other odd plants. Print out or draw pictures of them. Write a couple of sentences that tell about each plant. Make a book with the pictures. Read your book to a friend.